A Secret Princess

Bath New York Singapore Hong Kong Cologne Delhi Melbourne

Bath · New York · Singapore · Hong Kong · Cologne · Delhi · Melbourne

First published by Parragon in 2009

Parragon
Queen Street House
4 Queen Street
Bath BA1 1HE, UK

Adapted by Tracy Lake
Illustrated by Disney Storybook Artists
Designed by Kar Heng Goh
Printed and bound in Malaysia

A Secret Princess

Tracy Lake

Once upon a time, in a kingdom far away, a baby princess was born. Her parents named her Aurora, because they felt that she filled their lives with sunshine.

Soon after, a Christening ceremony was held for the new princess. The three good fairies brought gifts for baby Aurora.

Flora gave her grace and beauty.

Fauna gave her the gift of song.

But before Merryweather could bless the baby princess, they were interrupted …

All of a sudden, Maleficent the evil fairy appeared. She was angry that she hadn't been invited to the Christening. And so she enacted her revenge by cursing Aurora. 'When she is sixteen, she will prick her finger on a spinning wheel and die!' Maleficent roared.

Luckily, Merryweather had not yet given a gift to the baby princess. 'I can't undo Maleficent's spell,' she said, 'but I can change it. Instead of dying, you will fall into a deep sleep. Only the kiss of true love will break the spell.'

To protect Aurora, the fairies took her into the woods. There, they disguised themselves as peasants and raised the princess. To keep her identity a secret, they called her Briar Rose.

Briar Rose grew up in safety, not knowing that she was a princess and not knowing that she was cursed. She had a lovely voice that enchanted all of the woodland animals.

One day, a handsome prince named Phillip passed through the woods. When crossing the river, he fell off his horse. As he looked at his animal with great frustration, he heard a most beautiful voice.

Enchanted by the heavenly voice, Prince Phillip followed its sound. Before long, he came across a beautiful young woman.

The very moment that his eyes rested upon Briar Rose, Prince Phillip fell in love.

The young pair spent the rest of the day together, walking through the woods and singing to one another.

Briar Rose went back to the cottage and told the fairies about the handsome man. She had fallen in love!

The fairies decided it was time to tell Briar Rose that she was really named Princess Aurora and that today, on her sixteenth birthday, she was to return to the castle to be married.

Aurora soon arrived at the royal castle. But when she got there, Maleficent cast a spell that lured the princess to the castle tower.

Aurora entered the tower in a trance, and saw a spinning wheel. Her hand lifted, then reached out ... and she pricked her finger on the spindle.

The very moment that Aurora's finger touched the spindle, she fell into a deep sleep.

Flora, Fauna, and Merryweather knew that the kiss of true love could break the spell and that only Prince Phillip could save Aurora. But Prince Phillip had been imprisoned by Maleficent! And so the fairies set off to free him.

When the fairies found Prince Phillip, they gave him a magical sword and shield to fight Maleficent.

Prince Phillip soon found Maleficent. But when he confronted her, the evil fairy transformed herself into a giant, fire-breathing dragon!

While gallantly fighting the evil beast, Prince Phillip threw his sword at its heart. And as the sword plunged into the dragon, Maleficent was gone forever.

Prince Phillip quickly rushed to the sleeping Princess Aurora. He found her laid out on a bed, with a rose placed in her hands. Even asleep and under the spell, she looked beautiful. Prince Phillip leaned over and kissed her gently on the lips …

... and the spell was broken! Aurora awoke and embraced her prince. The couple were soon married, and everyone in the kingdom lived happily ever after.

The End